I am glad to be invited to talk to you all about my job. I am a caver.

I spend a lot of my time
underground. I explore for myself,
but not only that. I take people
down to visit caves, too.

The caves I love best are in Wales,
west of Brecon. I was there at the
weekend, taking some children
from a school in Usk.

We hiked up the hillside first,
to the mouth of the cave.

We stopped to slip and slide on the hard ground, which was slick with frost. It's important to have fun when you can!

We went inside in a line, single file, down into the complete darkness.

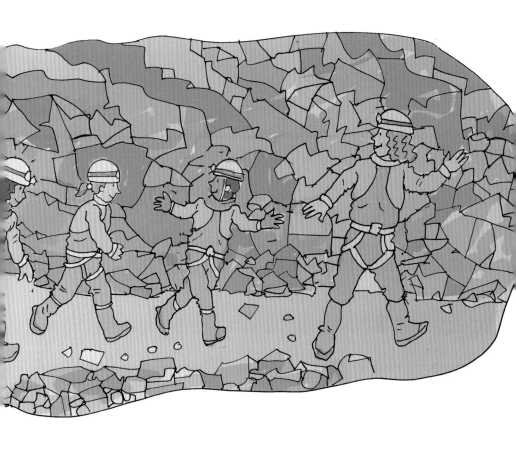

We all stood, still and quiet,
smelling the dank air and feeling
the chill from the walls of the
tunnel. It's hard to describe how
it makes you feel. It's like you've
stepped out of time.

After a while standing in the
dark, I turned on my torch.
The deposits of copper and zinc
always gleam and shine and glisten
under torchlight.

A girl asked if it was a mine.
I explained that mines are dug
out by people. These caves were
made by water running through
the ground.

Water can shift soil away and over thousands of years it even carves out the rock itself.

We walked on until the tunnel
opened out into a cavern.
Here it is on the slide.

You can see how wide it is, like a great hall. It's one of a string of chambers that we can walk through.

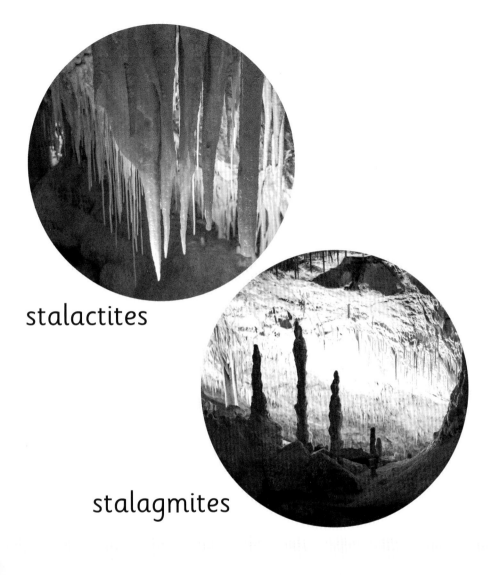

stalactites

stalagmites

On this slide you can see these
amazing rock shapes.
These ones are called stalactites ...
and these are stalagmites.

If you remember that tights hang down, that's stalactites.

Stalagmites rise up. Water drips and deposits the smallest mite of rock with each drop, far smaller than you can see.

I love it that caves move and are alive in this way. I love it that I get to be a caver!